In a high-rise building
deep in the heart of a big city
live two private eyes:
Bunny Brown and Jack Jones.
Bunny is the brains,
Jack is the snoop,
and together they
crack cases wide open . . .

This is the story of
Case Number 002:
THE CASE OF
THE CLIMBING CAT

story by
Cynthia Rylant

pictures by
G. Brian Karas

To Ian Frederick
—C. R.

For the Little Feet Library
—G. B. K.

Acrylic, gouache, and pencil were used for the full-color art.
The text type is Times.

The High-Rise Private Eyes: The Case of the Climbing Cat
Text copyright © 2000 by Cynthia Rylant
Illustrations copyright © 2000 by G. Brian Karas
All rights reserved.
Printed in Hong Kong
by South China Printing Company (1988) Ltd.
www.harperchildrens.com

Library of Congress Cataloging-in-Publication Data
Rylant, Cynthia.
The high-rise private eyes : the case of the climbing cat /
by Cynthia Rylant ; illustrated by G. Brian Karas.
    p.   cm.
"Greenwillow Books."
Summary: The High-Rise Private Eyes,
animal detectives, try to find the cat who
stole their neighbor's binoculars.
ISBN 0-688-16310-6 (trade).
ISBN 0-688-16309-2 (lib. bdg.)
[1. Animals—Fiction. 2. Apartment houses—Fiction.
3. Mystery and detective stories.]
I. Karas, G. Brian, ill. II. Title.
PZ7.R982 Ho 2000b   [E]—dc21 99-044210

1 2 3 4 5 6 7 8 9 10 First Edition

Contents

The Balcony

Bunny liked her balcony.

She tried to get Jack to sit on it.

"No, thanks," he always said.

"Oh, come on," said Bunny.

"Not in the mood," said Jack.

"Oh, come on," said Bunny.

"Nope," said Jack.

"It's not that high," said Bunny.

"It's twenty-two stories," said Jack.

"Pretend it's twenty-one," said Bunny.

"Are you hungry?" asked Jack.

"I think it's lunchtime."

"Are you changing the subject?"
 asked Bunny.

"Yes," said Jack.

"Chinese takeout?" asked Bunny.

"I'd prefer Mexican," said Jack.

"We'll get Mexican if you'll sit
on my balcony," said Bunny.

"Boy, I could sure go for
some chop suey," said Jack.

Chapter 2
The Case

Bunny and Jack got Chinese takeout.
Then they went
to Jack's apartment to eat.
Jack lived on the ground floor
of the high-rise.
"If you're afraid of heights,
why are you living
in a high-rise?" asked Bunny.

"I'm not afraid of heights,"
said Jack.
"Then why won't you sit
on my balcony?" asked Bunny.
(She was practicing
with her chopsticks.)
"It's chilly," said Jack.

"Jack, it's 94 degrees outside,"
 said Bunny.

"I'm delicate," said Jack.

"Ha," said Bunny.

"Could you pass the—"

The yell came from the hallway.

Bunny looked at Jack.

Jack looked at Bunny.

"Our lucky day!" said Jack with a grin.

Miss Nancy, the piano teacher,

was in the hallway, panting.

"What's up, Miss Nancy?"

asked Jack.

"Somebody stole my binoculars!"
 said Miss Nancy.

"Where were they?" asked Bunny.

"On my balcony!" said Miss Nancy.

"Don't you live on the twentieth floor,
 Miss Nancy?" asked Bunny.

"Yes," said Miss Nancy.

Bunny looked at Jack.

"Uh-oh," Bunny said.

Jack pretended not to notice.

"Then why are you down here
    on the first floor?" Jack asked.

"Because I chased him
    down the steps," said Miss Nancy.

"Chased who?" asked Bunny.

"The cat," said Miss Nancy.

"The cat with my binoculars."

"Where did he go?" asked Jack.

"I don't know," said Miss Nancy.

"He ran around the corner
  and disappeared."

"Hmmm," said Bunny.

"Jack," she said,

"you know what this means?"

"That that was some fast cat?"
asked Jack.

"No. It means we have to visit
the scene of the crime," said Bunny.

"On the twentieth floor.
On the balcony."

Jack thought about it.

"I feel chilly," he said.

"Maybe you should go without me."

"Oh, no," said Bunny. "We're on a case.

You have to be professional."

"Can I be professional

on *my* balcony?" asked Jack.

"You don't have a balcony," said Bunny.

"You have a yard."

"Exactly," said Jack.

They got into the elevator

with Miss Nancy.

It started going up.

"Is anybody hungry?" asked Jack.

When Bunny and Jack

got to Miss Nancy's place,

Jack had an idea.

"I'll check the steps," he said.

"Maybe the cat dropped a clue. See ya."

And before Bunny

could open her mouth,

he was off.

"Mercy," said Bunny, watching him go.

"Well, I guess I'm on my own.

Miss Nancy, may I see your balcony?"

"Certainly," said Miss Nancy.

"I do hope you can catch that cat."

Bunny stepped onto
Miss Nancy's balcony.
She looked around and wrote down
what she saw:

1 striped chair
1 pot of yellow roses
1 table with lemonade

"Would you like some lemonade?"
asked Miss Nancy.

"Thanks," said Bunny.

"It sure is hot today."

Meanwhile, Jack was going down
twenty flights of steps.
At number fifteen he picked up
a white feather.
"Hmmm," he said.
At number twelve he found
a ticket stub.
"Hmmm," he said.

Ten minutes later
he met Bunny at his apartment.
"I brought you some lemonade,"
said Bunny.
"Thanks," said Jack.
"I'm not sure you deserve it,"
said Bunny.
"I brought clues," said Jack.

He put the feather and the ticket stub
on the table.

"Hmmm," said Bunny, looking at them.

"Okay, you're forgiven."

"Hmmm," she said even louder,
thinking.

"What is it?" asked Jack.

"I've solved it," said Bunny.

"Already?" asked Jack.

"I haven't even finished my lemonade."

"Here are the clues," said Bunny.

"One set of binoculars, missing.

One white feather.

One ticket stub to the Aviary . . ."

"What's an aviary?" asked Jack.

"A place for birds," said Bunny.

CLues :

"*And*, the final clue, a balcony
   with a great view of the courthouse
   where all the pigeons live."
"I don't get it," said Jack.
"Birds. Binoculars," said Bunny.
"That cat is a birder."
"A what?" asked Jack.

"A bird-watcher," said Bunny.

"And bird-watchers will do *anything* to spot the bird they're looking for. Which explains why the cat was on the balcony."

"It does?" asked Jack.

"Sure," said Bunny. "That cat probably climbs around on balconies all day. Bird-watchers do a lot of climbing. The cat stopped on Miss Nancy's balcony. It was hot. And . . ."

"I've got it!" said Jack. "Lemonade!"

"Exactly," said Bunny.

"He was hot. He decided
   to have some lemonade.
   And he saw the binoculars."

"And *stole* them!" said Jack.

"Maybe not," said Bunny.

"Maybe he was just trying them out.
   Then Miss Nancy caught him."

"Why didn't he just escape
   by going down the way he came up?"
   asked Jack.
"You know cats," said Bunny.
"They hate climbing down.
   They have to think about it."
"So he ran through
   Miss Nancy's apartment
   and out into the hallway,"
   said Jack.

"Exactly," said Bunny.

"Aren't you glad I found those clues?"
asked Jack.

"Pleased as punch," said Bunny.

"Now let's go find the cat."

"Where?" asked Jack.

"The Aviary, of course," said Bunny.

"Oh, good," said Jack.

"I hope they have a gift shop.

I love gift shops."

"Concentrate, Jack," said Bunny.

"Right," said Jack.

"I wonder if they sell

those little snow globes?"

Chapter 4
Solved

*"S*now globes!" said Jack,

looking in the gift shop.

"Come on, Jack," said Bunny.

"Let's find the cat, then we'll shop."

Jack looked around the Aviary.

"Wow," he said. "So many birds."

"And bird-*watchers*," said Bunny.

"Let's go."

Bunny and Jack strolled
around the Aviary.
It was very big
with lots of hallways and special rooms.
"Wow," said Jack. "A bat room."
"Look for *cats*, not *bats*," said Bunny.
"Right," said Jack. "Wow, *parrots!*"

Bunny and Jack kept strolling.
Suddenly Bunny saw
something familiar.
"Look!" she said. "That cat has
a yellow rose in his lapel!"
"So?" said Jack.
"Miss Nancy had yellow roses
on her balcony," said Bunny.
"That's our man," said Jack.
"Let's go," said Bunny.

"Wait," said Jack.

"If he has binoculars,

   how will we know

   they're Miss Nancy's?"

"She told me they have MN on them.

   In pink," said Bunny.

"Got it," said Jack.

   They strolled over next to the cat.

"HMMM!" said Jack very loudly.

"AN INCREDIBLE SPECIMEN!"

"WHERE?" said Bunny, loudly.

"RIGHT THERE," said Jack.

"I CAN'T SEE IT," said Bunny.

"Oh, for goodness' sake," said Jack.

He turned to the cat.

"Would you have a pair of binoculars

my friend might borrow?"

he asked the cat.

"Certainly," said the cat.

He reached in his bag

and handed the binoculars to Jack.

"MN!" cried Jack. "*Gotcha!*"

It turned out that the cat indeed

had taken the binoculars.

But he never meant to keep them.

Miss Nancy had just frightened him.

He had planned to return
the binoculars to the balcony that night
when Miss Nancy was asleep.
Bunny and Jack believed him.
And this made the cat,
whose name was Seymour,
very happy.
He was so happy that he offered
to show them around the Aviary.

Seymour knew everything about birds.

Bunny and Jack were fascinated.

After the tour,

Seymour bought each of them

a gift at the shop.

Bunny got a mug.

And Jack got his snow globe.

Bunny looked at it.

"Now *I* feel chilly," she said.

"The cure for that

is to stay off balconies

and eat chop suey," said Jack.

So that's just what they did!

47

Bunny and Jack

and their new friend Seymour

returned the binoculars to Miss Nancy.

Then they all went out

for a Chinese dinner.

(On the ground floor.)